Where Are the Twins?

A Hiway Book

Where Are the Twins?

Rosemary Breckler

HIWAY

The Westminster Press
Philadelphia

First edition

Published by The Westminster Press®
Philadelphia, Pennsylvania

PRINTED IN THE UNITED STATES OF AMERICA
9 8 7 6 5 4 3 2 1

TO MY AUNT BEA
WHO HAS ALWAYS INSPIRED ME
TO PERSEVERE

Library of Congress Cataloging in Publication Data

Breckler, Rosemary, 1920–
  Where are the twins?

  "A Hiway book."
  SUMMARY: Two teenagers about to become full-fledged Police Cadets rescue twins lost in a rainstorm and mudslides and perform other helpful deeds too.
  [1. Adventure stories] I. Title.
PZ7.B744Wh   [Fic]   79–10390
ISBN 0–664–32651–X

Contents

1
The Longest Day

Carmen Chavez tried to see out through the steamed-up classroom window. It was still raining. Today was a very important day in her life. The rain could spoil it for her. She could hear the rain out there. It hit the window every little while. Sometimes it came with a roar. Other times it made a slapping sound. And sometimes it just sounded like tap-tap-tap or drip-drip-drip. What she wanted to know was, How hard was it raining?

"Carmen!" Miss Bray snapped at her. "I just asked you a question! You weren't even listening, were you?"

"No—uh-h-h," Carmen said. "I was worrying about the rain."

"And what good will worrying about the rain do?" Miss Bray asked. "Will that make it stop?" Her voice was very jumpy.

It had been like that all day long. Everyone

was mean and snappy because it had been raining so hard for six days without one dry day, or even one dry hour, to break the rain.

"The question!" Miss Bray yelled.

Carmen was trying to think what the question was. But her mind was blank. She had been thinking about the rain, and she had been keeping an ear tuned to the radio that Buff Bingham had hidden under his jacket. She could just barely hear it. He kept it tuned to the weather reports.

"I don't think I heard the question," Carmen said. "Would you please ask it again?"

Just then Buff moved in his seat and bumped the dial on the radio. The weather report came out loud and clear.

"More and more of the roads in the hills and canyons are being closed by mud slides and flooding," the newsman said. "Six days of rain have turned the hillsides into waterfalls of mud and rock slides."

"Turn that off!" shrieked Miss Bray. "You know you are not to bring radios into the classroom!"

"But I live high up on the side of the mountain," Carmen said. "And so do several others in this room. Please, Miss Bray, can't Buff keep the weather report turned on—low—so we can hear what is happening up by our homes?"

"I also live in the mountains," Miss Bray said,

"but I can't get any attention out of this class now. No. The radio must go. Buff, please, put it out in your locker and then hurry back. Did you hear me? I say hurry! We have a test to take yet this afternoon."

Miss Bray reached into her desk. "Carmen, please pass out these papers for the test."

Everyone groaned. There was a lot of mumbling.

"I think they should just close up the school and let us go home," Sara Green said. "Our minds are worn out from the rain. We can't think anymore."

"It's never going to stop raining," Will Taylor said very loud. "Someone ate too many beans and blew a big hole in the sky, that's what happened."

They all started laughing and yelling and stamping their feet. Miss Bray pounded a book on her desk.

"I didn't think that was the least bit funny," she said.

As Carmen passed out the papers, she could see out the window. The rain was coming down so hard that the tall trees out in front of the high school were bending their heads downward. They look as if they are crying, she thought. She felt a little bit like crying too.

For six months she had been looking forward to tonight. And now, with Buff's radio gone, she had no way of knowing if the canyon road was still open up to her house. It was a little road, called Snake Road. It wasn't very wide, and it curved back and forth, tight up against high cliffs, climbing up to the canyon high in the mountains where she lived.

She was really worried. Because of the rain, or the slides on Snake Road, her uniform might not be brought to her house today. Tonight was the meeting when she was going to get her pin. She had worked so long and so hard to get that pin!

She looked at the clock on the wall. Almost three o'clock. Already this had been the longest day of her life. And it still wasn't over. Now she had to take this dumb test. Then she would have to wait in the rain for the bus. It would be a big poke today, she was sure. On rainy days the driver always drove the school bus so slowly that she sometimes felt she could walk faster than the bus moved.

A big flash of lightning crackled across the sky. It lighted up the classroom. Sara Green clapped her hands over her ears. The thunder rolled through the sky and made the school feel as if it was shaking.

Miss Bray looked down at the test paper. Her face was white. I'll bet she wishes she could go home right now, Carmen thought, just like the rest of us.

Miss Bray turned and looked up at the clock. "We'll wait one more minute," she said, "for Buff to come back. We wouldn't want him to miss the test."

Carmen was wishing she could find a faster way to get home than that school bus. What if the uniform didn't get there in time? Would they put the pin on her anyway? But that wouldn't be as much of a thrill. The uniform just had to get there!

Was this day never going to end? Her ears were straining—waiting—listening for that final school bell to ring.

2
A Hint
of Trouble

Carmen placed her test paper on Miss Bray's desk and was on her way back to her chair, when the bell at last rang. She was the first one out of the room. She walked fast down the hall.

But when she got to her locker, two girls were standing there talking. They blocked her from her locker.

"Would you mind stepping over a little bit," she said. "I want to get into my locker."

A tall, thin girl turned around and looked at her.

"What's your hurry, Carmen?" the girl asked. Her voice sounded like a snake. It had a hiss to it.

Carmen looked at the girl. "I don't know you. How do you know me?"

"Hah!" The girl threw her head back. "We all know about you! If you think you're going to get away with any spying in this school—well, let me tell you, you're going to get your fat little cop's head busted in flat as a door!"

"Spying?" Carmen wasn't sure what the girl was talking about. "You mean because I'm going to be a Police Cadet? That's not what Police Cadets do."

"Oh, don't hand me any of that crap!" the girl said. "All fuzz are creeps and sneaks. Pigs and rats."

As she talked she had stepped a few feet away from Carmen's locker. Carmen opened the locker.

"Our training was to keep the peace," Carmen said. She set her umbrella against the locker next to hers and slid her arms into her raincoat. "We assist the police in lots of ways— but we're never mixed up in any busts."

"Lying fink!" the tall girl said and she picked up Carmen's umbrella, put it on the floor, and jumped up and down on it until it was broken.

At first, Carmen tried to pull the umbrella away from her. But then, Carmen looked at the other girl's eyes and saw that they were very large and too bright. From her training she knew the other girl was high on some kind of drug. She had been taught never to say or do anything to ruffle any persons who were high on a drug. She knew they could become wild over nothing. So she just stood there and played it cool. She could see that her umbrella was useless. It would never open again.

Carmen closed her locker and started to leave, but the girl followed her.

"Why don't you take this old umbrella and shove it down your throat," the girl said. "Then I'll know for sure you won't be able to fink!" She laughed. Her laugh sounded like "Haw! Haw!" Very much like a crow.

Other kids had gathered around them.

"What's going on?" a redheaded boy asked.

"Oh, I'm just telling this rat fink that she better not start any spying in this school, if she knows what is good for her," the tall girl said.

"Spying?" the redheaded boy asked.

"Yeah! She's a pig! A Police Cadet!"

"You mean we have a spy in our high school?" someone shouted.

"I'm not a spy," Carmen said. She kept her voice very calm. She had learned that in the Police Cadet training class called Crowd Control. She knew that a calm voice can cool down excited people. Sometimes it can slow down or even stop a riot.

Just then Dr. Gibson, the principal, pushed his way through the crowd. "What's going on here?" he asked.

"Nothing."

"Not one thing."

"Just minding our own business."

The voices answered from all directions. Carmen looked down at her broken umbrella. The principal looked down at it too.

"Did you hit someone with that?" he asked.

"She tried to hit me with it," the tall girl said. "But I was too quick for her. I knocked it out of her hand and jumped on it. No one's going to poke me with an umbrella!"

Dr. Gibson looked at the tall, thin girl. "What's your name? You're new, aren't you?"

"I'm Lisa Lang. I just moved here from the other side of the mountain. We don't have people like this Carmen in the school where I came from."

The principal moved his hand to show Carmen that he wanted her to come with him.

The crowd in the hall stood back and Carmen followed the principal down to his office.

"Now you've never made any trouble before, Carmen," he said as soon as they were alone. "What's going on now?"

"It's my Police Cadet training, sir," she said. "Lisa knew about it and said I was being planted in the school as a spy and a fink."

"That's right. I remember. You did complete the training, didn't you? I remember when you came to me and asked me to fill out your recommendation. I also remember that I told you your life might not be a bed of roses and caramel apples if you went ahead with the training." Dr. Gibson sat and looked down at his hands.

"I get my pin tonight, Dr. Gibson." Carmen's voice was happy and excited. "I can't sit here. I'll miss my bus!"

"But just a minute, Carmen. I must talk to you. I understand that Police Cadet training is not spy training, and I'm sure the police would never risk putting a girl in a spot where she could get hurt. But I must warn you. There is grass and angel dust being sold on this campus —and used too. Now you aren't going to go around snooping into that, are you?"

"Of course not!" Carmen was angry. "I'm not a narc! I'm a Police Cadet. We're trained to assist the officers, but we don't take the place of an officer. Mostly we run errands, help direct traffic at football games, and stuff like that. We study first aid. We give tours of the police station. We give talks to Boy and Girl Scouts who might be interested in joining the police force when they grow up. We're helpers—like Santa's elves. We work in the background."

Dr. Gibson tipped his head back and laughed. "That's the first time I ever heard there might be policemen working for Santa!"

Carmen laughed, but at the same time she was watching the clock. She was beginning to hope that that poky old bus was more poky than usual tonight.

"We don't do real police work, but we help the police with their work," she said very fast.

She was trying to hurry things up so she could race for the bus. "And we learn how to be very good police officers—if we decide to go into that work when we are of age."

She was shifting around on the chair. Why couldn't he just let her go? He knew she lived up in Larks Canyon and had to ride the bus. And he knew it was raining. But he opened his mouth and went on again.

"Well, I just don't want you running any risks here on the campus," Dr. Gibson said. "We try to keep a tight lid on people who are using drugs or selling drugs. And we keep a sharp eye out for knives. So far, this campus has been one of the cleanest in the city."

He stood up and began to walk up and down the room. "My word!" he said. "What a kettle of fish you could stir up if you did decide to play spy! You could get cut with a knife—or even worse. You won't do anything like that, will you?"

She shook her head. She was thinking about Bill. He lived up in the canyon, too, and he was getting his pin tonight also.

"Have you talked to Bill Parker this way too?" she asked.

"No. Not yet. But I will. You two must understand that I can't do anything more for you than I can for anyone else in this school. Now you have put yourselves in a bad spot. The students are going to make you feel like poison ivy. But you chose it for yourselves. I can't change the world. But I do admire you for your courage and the hard work that you had to put in to become Police Cadets. All I ask is that you do your Police Cadeting off the high school campus!"

She stood up. "Maybe someday you'll need us," she said. "Have you thought about that? We had to learn a lot of things during our training. We might come in handy if there was another earthquake around here. Now, please, may I go before I miss my bus?"

He looked up at her and grinned. "Good luck, Carmen. I like your spunk. And tell the same to Bill for me."

Then he waved his hand for her to hurry off to catch her bus.

3
Stranded

Carmen pulled her coat up over her head like a tent and ran out into the rain. She could see out the front of the coat through the gap between two buttons. But no matter where she looked, she saw not one bus. Every one of the buses had left for the day!

At first she didn't know what to do. She ran out to the curb. The rain pelted the top of her coat and ran down onto her face. She could hardly see. I'll have to call Mom, she thought, and she won't like that. It will mean she'll have to drag the twins out into the rain and come down Snake Road. Her mom didn't like to drive on Snake Road even on sunny days.

"It has too many twists in it and sharp turns that I can't see around," Mrs. Chavez always said. "And when you're going down, the road is so narrow at some places you are almost driving through the sky!"

If only she could call her dad, but he was off on police duty. She thought about calling Bill. Sometimes his dad would let him use their four-wheel-drive off-road car, but Bill always had to ask his dad first. And his dad was on police duty too. Besides, Bill might still be on that poky old bus somewhere.

What should she do?

Carmen turned and ran back into the school. She ran to the office. "I missed the bus," she said. "May I use the phone to call home?"

Mrs. Crick stood up and came to the counter. "I'm sorry but the thunderstorm killed our phones. Is there something I can do?"

"You mean the phones are *dead?*" Carmen couldn't think of any worse luck. "I missed the bus! I wanted to call Mom."

Mrs. Crick looked around the office. There was only one other person left in the room. "Where do you live?"

"Larks Canyon."

Mrs. Crick frowned. "Oh, dear. Way up there at the top of that nasty road. I'd be scared to death to drive you up there!"

"If it wasn't raining so hard," Carmen said, "I'd walk home. I've walked home up that road many times."

"It must be two miles," Mrs. Crick said, "and steep as a barn roof all the way."

Carmen started toward the door. "Well, I

guess, if I have to, I'll walk it today."

"No!" Mrs. Crick said. "There are rocks sliding down that road." She turned to a boy who was wheeling some files across the corner of the room. "Tom, we don't have to move all those files today. Why don't you drive this young lady home?"

The boy named Tom came over to the counter. He had long shaggy hair and very dirty fingernails. He looked like someone else that Carmen knew, but she couldn't think who it was.

"Where's home?" There was a slur to his voice. His eyes were bright. Too shiny. Carmen wondered why he was working in the office after school.

"Larks Canyon," she said.

"Always wanted to have a look-see up there," he slurred. "Why not today? But I have to pick up my sis. She'll have to ride up with us. That all right with you?"

Carmen was thinking about that slur in his voice and his too-bright eyes. She knew he was using some kind of drug. Maybe, in some way, on the ride home, she could talk to him about it and get him to leave drugs alone.

"I'd be very thankful for the ride," she said.

Mrs. Crick shook her finger at Tom. "Now you drive safely."

"Always do," he said. "Come on. Find Sis.

She said she would wait on the porch of the gym."

Carmen pulled her coat back up over her head and followed along behind him as he ran across the grass to the gym building. She could see a tall, thin girl, wrapped up in a raincoat, wearing a large rain hat and blowing cigarette smoke into the air.

When they reached the steps of the gym, Carmen knew who the girl was. Lisa Lang was Tom's sister!

4
A Wild
Ride

"Well, isn't this neat?" Lisa said when she saw Carmen with Tom. "What's the matter with you, Tom, don't you know who this chick is? She's a spy."

"A spy? What kind of a spy?" he said, staring at Carmen.

"A narc, stupid!" Lisa said as she spun her cigarette out into the rain. "A copper."

Tom stared at Carmen. "How come you go to high school?"

"I'm not a spy," Carmen said with a grin. "I'm a Police Cadet." She looked at his shiny eyes. "You don't have to worry about me. I don't bust anyone."

"Better not," he said. "No chick takes a ride from this dude and then busts him!"

Lisa looked at Carmen. "You still want us to drive you home?" There was a sneer in her voice. It hinted at danger.

"I don't have any other way of getting home," Carmen said. "I would be very thankful." She was feeling very upset inside. This day seemed to be going from worse to worst.

"Well, then, hop in," Tom said.

Carmen looked at the lowered body of the '65 Ford. It was bright purple, with a big red dragon painted on the hood.

It was dry inside. The windows were steamed up so badly she couldn't see out of them. There were no seat belts.

Tom jumped into the front seat and started the car up with a roar. "I got slicks on the back wheels. I wonder how they'll take Snake Road."

Lisa had just gotten into the car. She jumped back out of it. "You're not taking this dragon up Snake Road in this rain, are you? Your back end won't clear the mud in the road!"

"Gotta take this chick home," Tom said. "Get back in. I'm not gonna come back to school for you."

Lisa grumbled, but she got back into the car. "Some stupid dude, you are," she said to Tom. "Dragging us up there just for her."

Carmen sat back and tried to make her stomach stay still as Tom swung the car like a yo-yo around the sharp twists in the road.

Twice Lisa screamed, "You're gonna get us killed!"

Carmen's uniform. Her pin. The pinning

meeting tonight. Everything suddenly seemed far away. Tom is going to fly right over the cliff on one of these twists, she thought, and his car with our dead bodies in it won't be found until the middle of next week.

Lisa lit up another cigarette. It had a sweet, minty smell. She held it out to Carmen. "Want a drag? I dare you!"

"That's angel dust and mint leaves in that cigarette, isn't it?" Carmen said.

"It won't hurt you none," Tom said.

"You scared of it?" Lisa asked and blew smoke in Carmen's face.

The car slid to the edge of the road. It was a long way down to the bottom. But Tom turned the wheel sharply and they slid back onto the road.

"You're right. I am scared of angel dust. I know what it can do to people. I feel sorry for anyone silly enough to use it."

"Silly?" Tom turned to look at her and the car got caught up on a rock, skidded, slid. Then it started to move up the slippery road again.

"Do you remember Jim Wise? Did you know him? He drowned in the Colorado River on Labor Day," Carmen said.

"He was on the swim team, wasn't he?" Lisa asked. "How come he drowned?"

"Because he took a few puffs of angel dust before he dove into the river. It gets your mind all mixed up. He couldn't tell up from down, and he kept swimming down when he wanted to come up."

"Was he a friend of yours?" Lisa said.

"Yes." Carmen looked out the window. They were near the flat spot in the road that was the last place where a car could turn around. From there on up, the road was only half as wide and much steeper and twisted even more. "If you let me out here, I can run the rest of the way home. There's room for you to turn your car around here."

She stepped out of the car.

"You better not fink on us," Lisa said. "Or we'll turn every dude on you and bust your head."

Carmen shook her head. "I'm not a troublemaker! And, I thank you for the ride. Just think about Jim Wise once in a while."

She stood back to show Tom with her hands how much room he had for turning and backing the car. As soon as he was headed back down the hill, she turned and started to run up the hill. After everything else that had gone wrong that day, she really didn't expect her uniform to be there when she got home.

5
The Missing Twins

Carmen ran into the garage of her house and shed her muddy shoes and drenched coat. She wiped her face dry with one of the towels her mom had left on the washing machine, and then she wiped the mud off her legs. All the while, she was shaking inside. What was she going to do if the uniform wasn't there? She wasn't going to cry, was she? That was the way she felt.

As soon as she was dry and clean enough, she rushed into the house and to the hall table. A big box was there.

"My uniform!" she said. And she cried after all, but this crying was from joy. She just couldn't believe it was really in her hands as she hurried into her room to try it on. The uniform fit just right!

"Ooooh, at last," she said as she turned back and forth in front of her mirror. "After six months of hard training, now at last I'm a Police

Cadet. And tonight I'll get my pin. I'm so happy I'm afraid I'll explode waiting for tonight."

She looked out the window. It was still pouring, but she wanted Bill to see her in her uniform. The rain seemed to be coming down harder. Night seemed to be coming early. But she put on one of her dad's raincoats so her uniform would be well covered. She picked up another umbrella.

Then she ran up the hill to Bill's house at the top of the canyon road. She was very careful not to splash mud on her new uniform. She stayed in the middle of the road.

"Ta da!" she said when Bill opened the door.

"Ta da, yourself," he laughed. He had already put on his uniform. "But we're not real Police Cadets," he said, "until we get our pins at the meeting tonight."

Carmen hugged herself. "Oh, it seems like I've been waiting for tonight all my life!"

She walked around him, looking at his uniform and then down at her own. "It isn't too— uh-h-h—mannish for me, is it?" She looked up into his face.

Bill laughed. "It makes you look more like a girl than ever, my kind of girl." He reached down and touched her hand. She put her hand on top of his.

"I guess we're going to be spending even more time together, now, than ever," she said.

He gave her hand a little squeeze. "That's great with me." He held on to her hand for a minute while he smiled at her.

Carmen gave a big sigh. "You know, there was a time when I hated being a cop's brat. Now here we are, heading the same way."

"I had to punch a lot of kids when I was growing up," Bill said. "They would call me 'copper's snot.' I used to wish Dad was a doctor, or something like that. Then, I got thinking one day. A policeman is a kind of doctor. He tries to keep people safe and happy and well in his town or city."

"I know," Carmen said. "I've thought the same kind of things."

"But now I'm real proud Dad's a policeman. I'm glad we have this chance to follow in their shoes by becoming Police Cadets."

"Me, too. They're going to be so proud when they put our pins on us tonight." She grinned. "Then, after that, all we have to do is hope that something will happen that is more exciting than directing traffic at the football games."

"Oh!" Bill said as he gave her a playful punch. "You sound like you're hoping for some bad luck to happen around here or in the city."

"No. Not that. I just want a chance to do something important. More than giving blood to the blood bank and telling people where to park their cars."

Carmen and Bill lived in one of the rugged canyons high up the side of the mountains that cut Hollywood off from the San Fernando Valley in Los Angeles. They lived on the valley side.

Though they were still close to the city, the canyon was like a little town all by itself. In the mountains that surrounded them on three sides, and on the mountainside below, lived deer, rattlesnakes, coyotes, and hawks. Once in a while a wildcat would be seen.

Because the canyon was part of Los Angeles, their fathers had to serve in any part of Los Angeles where they were needed. And, so Carmen and Bill might be sent miles from the canyon. Most likely, though, they would work close to their homes.

While Carmen was talking, she was looking out the big glass window in the dining room of Bill's house. Behind his house the mountain went straight up like a wall. Mud was streaming down.

"I never saw so much mud come down the mountain," she said. "Bill, do you think we are going to have a flood? It's been raining hard for six days now."

"Up here?" Bill laughed at her. "There never has been a flood in Larks Canyon. The water all runs down into the valley. I heard on the radio that a lot of the streets down there are flooded.

They are asking people to stay home and not drive their cars."

"I hope it won't spoil tonight's meeting," Carmen sighed. Then she gasped. "Bill, look at the water! It's coming down into your backyard just like a big muddy waterfall."

"I've sure never seen it like this before. But I can't remember it ever raining this hard for so many days before in my life."

Just then the phone rang. It was Carmen's mother.

"Are Biff and Flory with you?" she wanted to know.

"No, Mom," Carmen said. "I ran up here alone. I was so excited! I couldn't wait to show my uniform to Bill! Besides, it's raining so hard. I wouldn't take them with me in this rain."

"Well, then, where can they be? I've looked all through the house. When did you last see them?"

"They were sitting in front of the television watching something about Santa Claus. That was when I came home and found my uniform," Carmen said.

"And I was in the attic looking through some old magazines for pictures their kindergarten teacher wanted," her mother said.

"Mom, I don't think they would have gone out in this rain. It's pounding so hard they would hardly be able to walk in it. They must be playing a trick on you again. They must be hiding somewhere in the house."

Carmen's mom gave a big sigh. "Those twins! They really wear me out. I get so sick of their tricks!"

"I'm sure they're just hiding, Mom," Carmen said. "They wouldn't go out in the rain."

"I suppose you're right. But I have already looked everywhere. I'll go around again." She gave another big sigh. "This is the worst rain I can remember. And . . . oh, I almost forgot. Captain Hope called a little while ago. Your meeting is called off for tonight."

"You mean," Carmen gasped, "after all we went through, we can't be sworn in and get our pins tonight? We still have to wait to become real Police Cadets?"

"Oh, Carmen, you've been a policeman's daughter all your life! You know that in a storm like this they are all needed on duty somewhere. They can't take time to hold a meeting."

Carmen gulped. "I just never get used to being a policeman's daughter. It's one disappointment right after the other."

"Well, now you've chosen it for your life too." Her mom's voice sounded as if she was trying to be cheerful. "Don't worry, dear, the storm will be over and the meeting will be held. Your dad will be one of the proudest fathers there. His fingers have been itching to put that pin on you ever since you went into training. A day or two won't make that much difference in your life."

"I'm still disappointed," Carmen said. "But right now I'll come home and help you find those twins. Try to think—where haven't you looked?"

"I told you! I've searched this house from top to bottom!" her mother said and then hung up the telephone.

Carmen looked at Bill.

"I know you think our twins are brats, but will you help me look for them, Bill? I have a sneaky feeling Mom is right. They aren't hiding in the house. They are somewhere . . . out in the rain."

"In this rain?" Bill said, shaking his head. "Two little kids five years old out in rain? I don't believe it. They must be hiding somewhere in your house."

"Wherever they are, we have to find them. Come on, put on your old clothes and we'll run down to my house and search the attic, closets, everywhere. Even under the house."

Bill looked up at the muddy waterfall. "There must be a river under your house!"

"That's what I'm scared of! Sometimes they hide under there!" Carmen had tears in her eyes.

6
Trapped

When they came running into the Chavez house, they found Carmen's mother crying. "They just are not here! Anywhere!"

Carmen was shivering. "That rain is getting like ice. They'll be sick if they're out in that rain," she said.

"Don't you think I know that?" her mother said. "I've been trying to call Captain Hope and have him send someone up here, but the phone is dead."

"But you were just talking to me," Carmen said. "And then you hung up."

"I didn't hang up. The phone went dead." Her mother looked out at the icy rain. "It's times like this that I hate being a policeman's wife! If only I could call your father at his office and ask him to come home and help us look! But a policeman is always out helping someone else, when his own family needs him most."

"Maybe he's back at the station now," Bill said. "Or they could get him on the radio?"

Mrs. Chavez looked sadly at Bill. "First, we can't make the telephone work. Second, even if the telephone would work and we called Captain Hope, we couldn't get in touch with Carmen's dad. There's some prince, from some country I never even heard of before, in Los Angeles today. My husband has the task of spending the whole day with the prince to be sure he is safe."

She went over to the stove and poured herself a cup of hot coffee. "That's something else that makes me mad. Every time some king or prince or big shot from some strange country comes to see Los Angeles, we taxpayers have to spend a big wad of our money. We have to feed them feasts, show them around town, and surround them with police to keep them safe. I'd rather spend our tax money on schools and hospitals. Why can't they take potluck and bring their own guards?"

Carmen looked at Bill. "This is something that always upsets Mom and Dad."

"Well, we people in Los Angeles pay more tax money to show our city to strange people than any other city in the country," her mom said. "And John draws that duty too often."

Carmen started toward the stairs. "I'll be

right back. I'm going to change into old clothes."

Bill tried the telephone. It didn't make any kind of sound at all.

When Carmen came down, she was dressed in the hip boots her dad had bought her when he took her on a fishing trip during Easter week. She was also wearing her heavy raincoat and hat.

"Dad said I might need this rain gear after I was a cadet," she said. She looked at her umbrella. "Maybe I'd better take the umbrella along for the twins when I find them."

Her mother was putting on her coat. "I'm coming with you!"

"Mom," Carmen said, "you can't. You were just in the hospital."

"But I can't just sit here and eat my fingernails while I wait!" her mother said.

"Mom, just tell me a couple of things. Where were Biff and Flory the last time you saw them?"

"Why . . ." Her mom was thinking. "Oh, I know. They were in the kitchen eating peanut butter, jelly, and crackers. Their teacher called and asked if I had any old magazines and I said I'd go through the ones in the attic. I turned the television on for them in the living room, but I told them they couldn't go in there until after they ate their crackers."

Carmen looked at Bill. "That must have been about ten minutes before I came home." Then she turned back to her mother.

"Mom, did you yell at the twins for anything this afternoon? You know—make them mad enough to want to run away or hide?"

Her mom looked at Bill. "Who can help but yell at those twins? They drive everybody crazy!"

"But, Mom. What did you yell at them about today?"

Her mother had to stop and think.

"Not much," she said after a while. "After I picked them up at kindergarten, come to think of it, they were pretty good today."

"All afternoon?" Carmen said.

Her mother bit her lip. "I can only remember one thing. When the mailman came, he rang the bell. He had your uniform. When I opened the door, the twins went out on the porch, and when they came back in, they brought a big, wet, muddy red dog in with them. It ran all over the living room rug and made mud everywhere. I shooed it out!"

"Whose dog was it?" Carmen said.

Her mother shrugged her shoulders. "I don't know. I don't remember that I ever saw it before."

"What happened then?" Bill asked.

"Why, I went to change the twins' clothes.

Then I went to fix their lunch. While they were eating, I cleaned up the mud."

"Mom, did you see what happened to the dog?"

"I think it went along with the mailman. I don't know. I never saw it again."

Carmen went over and opened the front door. Night had come early. Everything was wet and black. "There's someone running down the road," she said. "Maybe they know where the twins are." She strained her eyes to see. "It's Mr. Porter," she said, and she went out to meet him.

"Did you hear that roar?" he yelled. "The whole top of the mountain slid down on Adler Road. No way to get out the top of the canyon now. We're blocked in until someone comes to dig us out."

"But there's still the Snake Road that winds down into the valley," Bill said.

Mr. Porter shook his head. "Not anymore! You haven't been listening to the radio. That's been closed by a mud slide for more than an hour. We're all stuck in here. Fifty-five families. Fire engines can't get in. Police can't get in. We can't get out."

Carmen and Bill looked at each other.

"We've completed our Police Cadet training," she told Mr. Porter. "If anything happens, we might be able to help. But right now we have to find the twins. Mom was in the attic and they just disappeared right out of the house."

"You mean those two little ones are out in this rain?"

"Where do you think Biff and Flory might have gone?" Carmen asked Mr. Porter.

"Into somebody's house," he said. "Anyone seeing them out in the rain would have taken them in. Check around."

"The phones aren't working," Bill said. "We'll just have to go house to house."

"I wish I could help you," Mr. Porter said. "But I'm sure they are somewhere safe—and my house isn't. I have to hurry home and get a shovel. If I don't dig a trench around my house to guide the water away from it, I might lose my house."

Mr. Porter stood back from them. The mud was oozing all around his feet like a river of fudge. "You don't really think any harm has come to them, do you?"

"No," Carmen said slowly. "We'll find them. You go save your house."

Just then another loud roar came from somewhere on the mountain up above him.

"Another land slide," he said sadly and shook his head.

"Hurry!" Carmen said to Bill as she ran to the nearest house. "We've got to find Biff and Flory!"

7
Help

When they reached the first house, Carmen pounded on the door several times.

"The rain is making so much noise," Bill said, "I don't think they can hear us."

Carmen looked around the door. An old brass cowbell was hanging by a rope. "Maybe the Johnsons will hear this," she said, and she rang and rang the bell until it almost sounded like a fire bell.

The porch light came on. Mr. Johnson stood looking out the door at them. "Why are you out in this rain?" His voice sounded cross.

He opened the door very slowly. He had broken his legs at work two months before. He still limped and walked with a cane. "All this wet, days and nights of rain, are making my legs feel very bad. Why did you get me up from my chair and drag me to the door by ringing the cowbell?"

"The twins—my brother Biff and sister Flory
—are gone. They are out in the rain somewhere." She shouted above the noise of the
rain. "Have you seen them?"

"Those little kiddies out in this rain!" Mr.
Johnson looked down at his feet and the cane.
"I'd come out and look for them if I could,
b-b-but . . ." His voice was sad.

"We understand, Mr. Johnson. One of these
days you'll be just as well as ever. We have to
hurry now. Are you sure you didn't see them
this afternoon?"

"You mean they have been gone that long?"
He shook his head. "No, the only thing I saw
this afternoon was that big red mutt that was
romping along with the mailman. Have you
phoned around?"

"Our phone is dead. How is yours?" Carmen
asked.

He left them for a minute. Then he came
limping back to the door. "Dead too."

"If you see the twins, Mr. Johnson," Carmen
said, "will you keep them here with you until we
get back?"

"Sure."

Then Carmen and Bill were racing down the
canyon to the next house. All the houses were
far apart.

"Old Mrs. Hale will never come to the door
on a rainy night like this," Carmen said as she

stopped at Mrs. Hale's door and pressed on the bell.

"But we can't take a chance," Bill said. "We have to go to every house. You never know what people will do when it is raining this hard and the phones are dead."

Bill was looking around the side of the house. "If Biff and Flory went out through your back gate and came around the bottom of the hill, this would be the first house they would see."

A light tapping on the window glass next to the door made them look that way. Old Mrs. Hale, wearing a warm robe, was tapping on the glass. She was telling them to go away.

"Maybe she doesn't know us," Carmen said.

"She knows," Bill said, "but she doesn't want to open the door and let the cold draft blow in."

Carmen looked down at the wet mud near her feet. She used the umbrella like a pen. She wrote: TWINS ARE LOST. SEEN THEM?

Old Mrs. Hale shook her head no. Then she made some words with her mouth and walked away from the window.

"Doesn't she know we can't hear her through the window?" Bill said. "What do you think she said?"

"Oh, I could read her lips! She said, 'I expected it!' She never liked Flory and Biff." Carmen bit her lips. "They sometimes picked her roses. She told Mom once that they should be kept tied up like puppies until they learned where to stay. Out of her yard, is what she meant."

"Then why doesn't she put up a fence?" Bill wanted to know.

"I don't think she has that much money," Carmen said. She was looking up the hill. The rain was coming down harder and harder.

"Wouldn't you think the sky would be empty by now?"Carmen said, shaking rain from her hat.

Bill was looking down the road. "It would be faster if we split up. For the rest of the way down this road, I'll go to the houses on the east and you go to the houses on the west. Then we'll meet by that big rock down there at the end of the road—if we haven't found Flory and Biff by that time."

Carmen was looking down at the big rock. It was hard to see it in the rain and the dark. "When we were little kids we used to hide behind that rock, remember?"

"But not when it was raining," Bill said. "There's not a dry spot there. Let's go! Hurry!"

But it was the same at every house. No one had seen the twins. Some of the men wanted to help look, but Carmen and Bill saw how busy they were with shovels. They were out in the mud digging trenches to save their houses. If they stopped digging and the mud piled up against their houses, they might not have a home. And then, what if the twins were found watching television at someone's house?

She shook her head. "Not yet. We'll come back and get you if we need help. We still think they are in one of the houses near here."

"We'll be here if you need help," the men said. Most of them were wearing boots and raincoats. "We won't stop digging until it stops raining—unless you need help."

8
Not One Clue

Carmen looked back up the hill toward her own home. She wondered where her dad was by now. That prince should be on his plane flying back to his own country by this time. Or was the rain keeping him here? Would Dad have to stay with him?

Her father was always so glad when their planes flew the visiting kings, princes, and important people back to their own countries. Then he would hurry home.

If Dad was off duty, was he on the other side of one of the slides that were blocking the roads? Was he with men who were trying to dig one of their roads open? Carmen began to wish she had a CB radio, but she wasn't sure it would work in this storm in this deep canyon so high in the mountains. Sometimes the picture on their television was very poor, and their radio sounded scratchy.

She tried to listen. She tried to hear whether any heavy earth-moving machines were working to get the mud off the roads. But all she could hear was rain.

She had stopped at every house on her side of the road when she heard another loud roar. Then she heard loud voices. They sounded excited. She ran across the road to Bill.

"What happened now?" she asked him.

"I think another big chunk of mountain fell."

Tears came to Carmen's eyes. "I don't know where to look anymore," she said. "I'm frightened. What if the twins went higher up the canyon and were hit by one of the mud slides?"

"That's where we are going to look now," Bill said. "Along the little side roads that cut across this road above your house."

"They don't go up there very often, Bill. The road is so steep. It's a hard climb for them."

"Well, that's where we have to head now. They have to be in someone's house up there," he said.

Then Carmen remembered. "Susie lives up there! Mom used to drive them up there to visit with her. Why didn't I think of that before? Mrs. Feder would keep them there in this storm. I don't know why they would climb all the way up there in the rain, but I'll bet that's where they are. Hurry!"

But Bill didn't move. He was looking at Carmen. "Are you sure Mrs. Feder would let them stay at her house? Don't you remember last week? You were very mad at Mrs. Feder."

"Well, that was because she yelled at Mom. And Mom was just home from the hospital. She told Mom the twins were awful brats. She said they nearly drove her crazy every time they came to her house. She asked Mom to keep them home."

"So that doesn't sound like a good place to look," Bill said.

"Oh, but yes it is! Two days later she said Susie was so lonely *she* was driving her crazy. Mrs. Feder asked Mom if she could come down and get the twins. She took Biff and Flory up to her house to play with Susie again. So you see," Carmen said, "it was all right again. People change from one day to the next. It all goes by how they feel."

"Everybody has bad days sometimes," Bill said.

They tried to hurry through the mud, the rain, and the dark that had closed in on the canyon. The road was very steep and very slippery.

"It's worse than climbing up a sliding board," Carmen said. "So much mud is sticking to my boots my feet are almost too heavy to lift."

They stopped and scraped some of the mud

off their boots. Then they started up the road again.

When they rang the doorbell Mrs. Feder yelled, "Come in!" They wiped the mud from their boots and walked into her living room. She was standing on the other side of the room, close to the big glass windows. She was looking up at the mountain behind her house.

"Look!" Mrs. Feder pointed up at the mountain. Then she screamed.

Carmen and Bill ran to her side. They looked up at the place where Mrs. Feder was pointing. A big tree was starting to move down the mountain. It looked as if it was sliding on skis. It moved very slowly.

"That tree is going to slide right in through this window!" Mrs. Feder screamed.

Carmen and Bill held their breath as they watched the tree. It kept coming, slowly, inch by inch, straight toward them. A lot of mud and rocks were coming with it. It started to move faster. There was a loud roar. The tree, the rocks, the mud all landed in a big heap in Mrs. Feder's backyard. But the mud slide stopped about three feet from the window glass.

Mrs. Feder was so scared, she sat right down on the floor. "The whole mountain tumbled into my backyard!" she said and she hid her face in her lap.

"What can we do for you?" Carmen said. She rubbed Mrs. Feder's hands with her own hands. Carmen's hands were cold. But Mrs. Feder's hands were colder.

Carmen stood up. "Would you like a nice hot cup of tea?"

Mrs. Feder nodded her head. Carmen made the tea very strong.

"Here, drink this," she said to Mrs. Feder. "It will make you feel better."

Mrs. Feder drank the tea. She did seem to feel better by the time she had drunk all the tea in the cup. She looked toward the bedrooms. "That big roar didn't even wake Susie up!"

"The rain has been making as much noise as a train," Bill said. "What is one more roar to a little girl when she's asleep?"

"Four-year-olds can sleep through any-thing," Carmen said. "When they are tired."

She looked at Mrs. Feder. "We can't find our twins! That's why we came here. Have you seen them this afternoon?"

"No. And on a day like this I wouldn't have invited them in. I would have driven them straight home to your mother. Susie was wild enough for me to handle today. Ugh! I hate rainy days!"

Mrs. Feder was trying to get up and Bill helped her.

"I like Biff and Flory," she said as she stood

up. "They have nice manners and they are very sweet children. But, sometimes when they play with Susie, I almost go out of my head!"

"They get a little wild sometimes," Carmen agreed. "And, they always stick together."

"Gang up on another child you mean!" Mrs. Feder sputtered. "Why don't you call around? They must be driving somebody else crazy."

Carmen shook her head. "We can't. The telephones are dead."

"You mean I can't call my husband to hurry home? We must both get out of this house before the mountain falls on top of it!"

"The roads are blocked by mud slides too. He couldn't get home if he tried."

"You mean I have to stay here with Susie and just wait for that mountain to kill us?" She started to scream again and Carmen went to get her another cup of tea.

Mrs. Feder kept screaming, "I can't get out of here!"

Bill helped her over to the sofa and she stretched out on it. He went and got a towel. He wrung it out in cold water and pressed it against her forehead.

"Take it easy, Mrs. Feder," Carmen said. "You can always drive down to my house. You and Susie will be safe with Mom. The mountain doesn't come close to our house."

Carmen gave her more tea. Mrs. Feder drank some of it. Then she looked at Carmen and Bill. "Where are your dads?"

"My dad is on duty," Carmen said. "He was sent to guard some prince who is in town."

Mrs. Feder set her cup down very hard. She spilled some of the tea. "That's just it! Why isn't he here protecting the people who pay him? I'm a taxpayer! That prince is not!"

She turned to Bill. "Where's your dad?"

"He's on duty somewhere too."

"I knew it," Mrs. Feder yelled. "We have two policemen living in our canyon, and when we need them they are always somewhere else. What do we pay taxes for?"

"We are both Police Cadets," Carmen said. "We've had our training. We know how to help."

Mrs. Feder looked at them. "Two kids! You'd be about as much good as that big red dog that was following the mailman today."

Carmen looked at Bill.

"That big red dog again. Why is it that everyone has seen the big red dog, but no one could see two children?" Carmen wondered.

"Ish!" Mrs. Feder made a face. "You should have seen that dog! Rolling over and over and over in the mud out by the road. He looked like a great big strawberry fudge sundae."

Carmen and Bill started to leave. Mrs. Feder followed them to the door.

"Then the dog ran after the mailman and the rain washed him clean. He was bright red."

9
A Giant Bat

Bill stood in the center of the road. The night was very dark. The rain still pounded down. He looked at the mountaintops around them.

"I don't think we can go any farther on foot," he said. "Let's go back to my house and get Dad's off-road car."

Carmen looked at him. "Even that might get stuck in this mud."

"But we'll just have to risk it," he said. "All the houses above here are too far apart. We can stay on the roads. They are so steep. They must have more water on them than mud."

"How in the world could Biff and Flory go higher up the canyon than this? They have such short, chubby legs," Carmen asked.

"Kids can do some funny things." Bill stopped talking and looked up the steep road above them. Car headlights were coming down very slowly toward them.

"Maybe someone has the twins!" Carmen shouted.

They waited for the headlights to come to them. It seemed to take hours.

When the car reached them it stopped. It was the Besses' station wagon. The Besses lived almost at the top of the canyon. Mrs. Bess rolled her window down. They could see that the car was packed with clothes and books and a camera was on top of it all.

Carmen walked up to the window. "Our twins are missing. Have you seen them?"

"The twins . . . out in this?" Mrs. Bess looked as if she didn't believe them. "Don't you watch them better than that?" she scolded. "Why they could die in the mud!"

"We know!" Carmen had tears in her eyes. "We've been looking for them for hours."

"That long?" Mrs. Bess shook her head. "I've been up and down this road four times now. I haven't seen them. The mountain caved in on my house. I'm moving what I can save down to my sister's house. You know—she lives in that stone house above the wash."

"That doesn't sound like a very safe place. That wash is full of water to the top and roaring like a waterfall," Bill told her.

Mrs. Bess bit her lip. "I know. But it is safer than my house, and my sister's house isn't right on the wash." She swallowed hard. "You don't think . . . your twins . . . ''

Carmen shook her head. "No. From the time they could walk Dad told them never to go near the wash, and they couldn't climb the fence if they did. There's barbed wire on top of it."

"Still," Mrs. Bess said, "you never know what those two would do. And the rain might have washed out the fence. Haven't you checked down there?"

"We're getting my dad's off-road car right now," said Bill. "First we're going up the canyon to the very top, and then we'll drive down to the wash."

"Well, I'll keep my eyes open. I'll be driving up and down the road as long as I can. That is —as long as my car doesn't run out of gas and my house is still up there." Mrs. Bess began to let the car roll.

Carmen stepped back. But she shouted, "Are you sure you haven't seen anything that showed the twins had been there? Little footprints in the mud? Something like that?"

"No." Mrs. Bess shook her head. "The only odd thing I've seen tonight was a giant black bat."

"A giant black bat?" Bill shouted.

"Yes. It was very large, and it was down in the bushes," she said.

"What would a big bat be doing in the bushes?" Carmen wanted to know.

"Maybe the rain hurt its wings," Bill said. "Maybe it couldn't fly anymore."

Carmen poked her head into Mrs. Bess's car. "Are you sure it was a bat? Everyone else has said they saw a big red dog. But no one has seen a bat."

"Oh, the dog. Yes, I saw that two times. Come to think of it, I saw it just before I saw the big black bat. I think the bat was following it," Mrs. Bess said.

Carmen's face went very white. "Would a big bat eat a big dog?"

Bill shook his head. "I don't think so. But I know what you are thinking, Carmen! You must not think about a thing like that! I know the twins are safe somewhere in someone's house!"

Mrs. Bess started to roll up the window. "Now you have me scared! The bat was big and black and shiny." She drove off down the mountain road.

Carmen's knees started to shake. "A bat! A bat!" she yelled. "We've never had a bat in the canyon before." She started to shake all over until Bill reached over and put his arms around her.

"It's going to turn out all right, Carmen," he said. "Just hang in there. We're going to find the twins safe and sound."

It felt so good with his arms around her. He had never done that before. For a long minute she just stayed there, and she felt so safe. The nightmare of the rain and of Biff and Flory being lost seemed to dim. Bill's arms were so strong and warm. But she shook herself free.

"We aren't going to find them by standing here."

When she stepped away from him the night felt so much darker and colder.

10
A Long Delay

They stood still for about a minute. They were staring after Mrs. Bess's car. Then Carmen shouted, "Hurry! We have to get your dad's car!"

Carmen ran down the road as fast as she could. The muddy water sucked at her boots and slowed her down. Her heart was beating very fast.

She was thinking about the bat. When they got the car, they would have to stop by her house and tell her mother that they still had not found the twins. But they must not tell her about the bat!

Bill ran even faster than Carmen. He reached his house and ran inside to get the car keys. By the time she got there, he was already opening the garage doors.

As soon as he backed the car out of the garage, Carmen hopped into it. "We have to stop and tell Mom we haven't found them yet," she said.

Bill drove to her house. "Wouldn't it be great if your mom had the twins with her?"

Carmen smiled and jumped out of the car. She ran into the house. Her mother was standing by the window staring out at the rain. She was crying. "You haven't found Biff and Flory, have you?" she asked.

"No, Mom. But we have Officer Parker's off-road car now. We're going to the top of the canyon," Carmen said. "Then we'll go to the main canyon road and up as far as the big mountain slide."

Carmen looked at her mother's coffeepot. It was still bubbling. "Why don't you have another cup of coffee?" she asked her mother.

"Ugh! I'll throw up if I drink one more cup," her mother said. "You and Bill hurry along. I'm counting on you, Carmen. Right now you two are the only hope I have!"

The car sped up the wet road they had just run down. "It sure beats walking," Carmen said.

"Let's just hope we don't get stuck in the mud up there."

They were passing Mr. Porter's house, when Bill hit the brake.

"Why are you stopping?" Carmen wanted to know.

"I thought I saw something over there near the ground. Something black that was moving." The car had a searchlight. Bill turned it on and pointed it to the spot.

"It's Mr. Porter," Carmen said. "He's buried in the mud!"

Bill backed the car into Mr. Porter's driveway and parked. They both jumped out and ran to Mr. Porter.

He looked up at them. "I was digging the mud away from the house, but it came at me faster than I could dig."

"Where's your shovel?" Bill asked.

"It's somewhere around. The mud knocked it out of my hands and it went ahead of me. I think I can see the handle over there by Carmen. But if that's not it, there is another one in the garage. And I think Mrs. Brown, in that brick house across the road, has one."

Mr. Porter put his head down on the mud to rest. He was breathing very hard. Carmen wondered if he was having a heart attack.

Reaching down in the mud, she found the shovel. She pulled it out. It was a mess but it was not broken. Bill grabbed it from her. "Hurry! Get the other shovel. I'll start digging him out with this one."

But when she got inside the garage she could not find the other shovel.

She looked across the street. Mrs. Brown

lived there with her son, Pink Eye. He was a big bully. Everyone called him Pink Eye because the whites of his eyes were always red. Carmen wasn't afraid of him. She felt sorry for him. She knew his eyes were always red because he never got much sleep. His mother was always drunk, and he was afraid of her. To get even, he was mean to everyone else.

Carmen knew his real name was Carl, but he didn't mind being called Pink Eye. He liked to sound scary to little kids. She wished there was somewhere else she could go to get a shovel.

But she crossed the street and pressed hard on the bell. In Police Cadet training they were told always to speak softly and gently to drunks or bullies. She wondered which one would answer the doorbell.

It was Pink Eye. "What are you doing out in the rain, Stupid Head?" he asked.

"I need to borrow a shovel. Mr. Porter is buried under the mud," she said as calmly as she could.

"That old bird?" he said, and laughed.

"Please," Carmen said. "Do you have a shovel? We have to hurry and get him out. He's breathing very hard. And then we have to find our Biff and Flory. The twins are missing."

From behind Pink Eye came a scratchy voice. It sounded like a witch. "Carl, chase them away! We don't want anyone coming around here tonight! Tell them to go get lost!"

Pink Eye turned his head toward the voice. Then he turned back to Carmen. "I hear you're a fuzz-fink cadet now," he said.

"Please! All I want is to borrow a shovel," Carmen said.

"But I don't hate you," Pink Eye said. "You've always been nice to me. Wait. I'll get my raincoat and the shovel. It's boring here tonight. I'll help you dig."

While Pink Eye and Bill were digging Mr. Porter out of the mud, Carmen looked through Mr. Porter's garage again. This time she found the other shovel. It was behind a ladder. She pulled it out. Then she helped dig too.

When they got all the mud off, Mr. Porter didn't seem to be hurt. "I just want a hot shower and then I'll go to bed," he puffed.

"Are you sure you will be all right here alone?" said Carmen.

"He won't be alone," Pink Eye said. "I'll stay over here and watch his television. It's more peaceful than at my house."

Carmen wasn't sure that she should trust him. He looked at her as if he knew what she was thinking. "I'm used to taking care of sick people," he said. "For Pete's sake! I live all the time with one."

Carmen nodded. "You can do a better job at that than I can. But now we have to find the twins. You didn't see them this afternoon did you?"

Pink Eye looked at her. "If you hadn't been so nice to me, I wouldn't tell you."

"Tell us what?" Bill asked.

"Well, I'm not sure it was the twins. I only saw it from the corner of my eye," Pink Eye said.

"Saw what?" Carmen wanted to know.

"Well, I saw something following a big red dog. It was raining hard. I thought it looked like two little kids."

"Where?" Carmen cried.

Pink Eye pointed up the canyon. "They were headed toward the top."

11
A Very Strange Sight

Bill and Carmen had to slow down when they came to Mrs. Bess's house. The mountain had fallen against the back of it and pushed the house about four feet into the road. Otherwise, the house looked just the same as it always had.

"Good golly!" Carmen yelled. "It looks as if the house is walking across the road!"

Bill swung the car around it. "When we come back, we'll have to put a danger sign on that. It could fall on someone, but no one's out right now."

"Oh, is that so? There's a car back there moving as if a monkey is at the wheel." Carmen was looking back at the swinging and swaying headlights.

Bill couldn't look back. The mud was so deep that the four-wheel-drive car was having a tough time going up the mountain.

"Come on, Mud Hog," he yelled at the car,

"keep moving. You can make it! And we're too tired to walk any more tonight."

As if the car heard him, it moved a little faster. Carmen watched the mirror. They both could hear the car behind them tooting its horn. It was driving all over the road in zigzags.

"Aren't things bad enough," she said, "without having a creep following us?"

Bill swung his head around for a quick look, and then he slowed the car. "It's Mrs. Bess. Maybe she has seen the twins." He stopped and waited for her to catch up to them.

"My sister's house just washed off the hill," she said. "Now it's piled in the land slide on Snake Road. The wash just filled all the way up and flowed out of its banks and washed everything ahead of it right down the mountain. I always wondered why they called that gully a wash. Back in Ohio, where I come from, we have rivers, creeks, brooks, streams, and gullies, but no washes."

Carmen could see that Mrs. Bess was shaking all over. There was someone huddled under a blanket on the seat beside her.

"Washes are very bad. They are made by flash floods. They can be dry for years and when they fill with water they are killers of anything that gets in their way," Carmen said.

While Carmen talked she was watching the blanket. It moved. Mrs. Bess patted the blanket.

"My sister is under here. She is so afraid. She wants to go up and stay with Sara Mitchell, her best friend. Sara lives way up at the top by the water tower. My car can't make this hill. When I saw your four-wheel-drive car, I thought you might take her up there for me."

The blanket moved again. A little old lady with white hair and very frightened eyes looked at Carmen.

"I lost everything I ever had," she said. "But I'm still here."

"Have you found the children yet?" Mrs. Bess asked.

"No." Carmen shook her head.

"They're kidnapped," Mrs. Bess moaned. "I know it. I feel it. How many more things can go wrong tonight?"

Bill bent his head down. "Why do you think they have been kidnapped?"

"Because Carmen's dad is a cop," Mrs. Bess said. "Cops arrest people, and people want to get even with them. Oh, those poor children!"

Carmen opened the back door of their car. "Come on, Mrs. Bess," she said. "Help your sister into this car. We'll take you up to her friend. It's where we are headed."

After the women were in the car, Bill pressed the gas pedal all the way to the floor to get the car moving again in the mud.

"We don't believe the twins are kidnapped,"

he said. "We think they followed a big red dog up the canyon and got lost."

"The dog!" Mrs. Bess let out a yell. "The big black bat was after the dog! Maybe it got the twins too!"

Carmen looked at Bill. He was pressing down hard on the gas pedal. She was glad they were moving up the mountain fast. She didn't think she could stand to be with Mrs. Bess very long.

The rain seemed to split. For a minute it seemed as if someone parted the rain, like pulling back drapes. Way up ahead Carmen could see the big hulk of the water tower. Then the rain came down hard again, blotting it from view. There were no houses on this stretch of road.

"Sara's house is the only house left," Carmen said. "What is she like? I don't think I know her."

"She is very old," Mrs. Bess said, "and she has been very sick. I don't know how I will tell her that Sister's house washed into the mud slide. I don't want to frighten her. But we have nowhere else to stay."

There was a car port right by the side door. Bill drove into it. "Now you can get into the house without getting wet." He touched the horn. A light came on in the car port. The side door opened. A very tiny, white-haired lady stood looking out at them.

Carmen frowned. The old lady did look very frail. "Maybe you could wait until morning," she said. "When the rain has stopped, it might not be so hard to tell her."

Mrs. Bess shook her head. "I could never live through the night without telling her. And I don't think the sun will ever shine again." Her voice was getting higher and higher. "I think it is just going to keep on raining until we all wash right down into the valley and there will be no more homes or people up here in the canyon."

Carmen put her hand on Mrs. Bess. "Try to be calm," she said. "It will end. This canyon has been here for a long, long time. And, it will still be here for a long time. Now go on in and visit with your friend."

Carmen got out to help Mrs. Bess's sister into the house.

"What is taking you so long?" Sara called out to them.

Mrs. Bess stumbled as she got out of the car. Carmen helped Mrs. Bess and led her and her sister up the step to the door, where Sara was waiting.

"What a nice night to have a party," Sara said. "I baked some cookies this afternoon to chase away the gloom, and I have some lemons to make lemonade. Come on in, all of you." She held the door open wide.

"We can't," Carmen said. "But we'd like to come some other time. Right now we have to find my little brother and sister. They're twins. And they are lost."

"Twins did you say? How big?"

Carmen could hardly believe her ears. "Do you mean you have seen them?"

Sara looked at her and then she pointed at the car. "I don't know. How far will that searchlight reach?"

"About twenty feet," Bill said. "Maybe it will shine a little farther. Why?"

Sara waved with her hand for them to follow her. She led them to her rocking chair in front of a big window. "I'm a bird watcher," she said. "And this afternoon, just as it got dark, I saw something strange up under the water tower. It looked like a big black bat. So I watched it with my bird glasses. But it was the strangest bat I've ever seen."

She handed the bird glasses to Carmen. "Look under the tower. Can you see anything?"

"Not in the rain and the dark," Carmen said.

"Young man, could you turn the searchlight up there?" Sara asked.

Bill ran out to the car, backed it and drove as near to the water tower as he could. Then he turned the searchlight beam at the tower.

Sara looked through her bird glasses.

"Mighty odd bird." She handed the glasses to Carmen.

"It does look like a-a-a bat," Carmen said slowly. "But I didn't know bats had eight legs."

Sara took the glasses back from her. She looked into them for quite a while. "Doesn't it look as if four of the legs are brown and four are red?" She handed the glasses back to Carmen.

Carmen's eyes were getting used to the glasses now and she could see better. "Four muddy, chubby legs!" she shouted. "And four red furry legs—under the big black rubber cape Dad used to wear when he was a traffic cop!"

12
A Crack in the Mountain

Carmen was giving the bird glasses to Sara, when suddenly the floor started to shake. They all looked at each other. There was a loud rumble.

"Earthquake!" Mrs. Bess screamed.

"No. Another land slide, somewhere," Sara said. "They all feel like that up here."

"I've got to get up to Biff and Flory," Carmen shouted. She ran out through the front door.

Bill was slowly backing the car down toward Sara's house.

"No!" Carmen called to him. "We have to go up to the water tower."

"We can't," he said when he braked the car beside her. "A big crack opened in the mountain. It is too wide to drive across, and it spreads as far as I can see from left to right."

"Oh, no." Carmen's knees felt very weak. "What can we do now? You saw them, didn't you? The big black bat is my dad's old traffic rain cape with the twins and that big red dog hiding under it to keep dry."

"I saw a big black lump up there, but I couldn't tell what it was. Are you sure it is Flory and Biff?" Bill asked.

"I saw them with Sara's bird glasses," Carmen said.

Bill looked around the mountain. The rain was coming down more softly, but he could not believe it would stay that way.

"This mountain is as soft as mashed potatoes between here and the tower, and there is the long crack, spreading wider all the time. The only way I can see to get up to the twins is to find two wide boards. Then we will have to belly it up to the tower, pushing the boards in front of us. We can use the boards to get across the crack."

"Belly it?" Carmen yelled. "In this mud?"

"You did it in Cadet training," Bill said.

"But that was on dry sand on a warm day." Carmen looked down at the mud. "Yuck!"

"Hunh!" Bill said. "I guess you don't really want to get your Police Cadet pin—or save the twins. You just want to keep your belly warm and dry."

"Is that so?" she said. "Let's find the boards and see who gets up to the twins first! Don't forget. They are my little brother and sister."

Sara was waiting for them when they ran into the car port. "What can I do to help?" she asked.

"We need boards," Carmen said. "We have to push them across the crack so we can get the twins down the mountain."

Sara walked over to the corner of the car port. She opened a little closet and pulled out two boards. They were well wrapped in cloth. "Would these do?" she said as she pulled the cloth off them. "These are solid oak. They are part of my dining room table. They make it longer when I have a dinner party."

Carmen looked at the lovely wood. "Are they the only boards you have?" She hated to use anything that had been loved and well cared for over many years. "We will scratch them all up."

"Oak is very strong wood," Sara said. "And what better use could there ever be for them than to save the lives of two little children?"

She handed one board to Carmen and one to Bill.

He stood looking down at the boards and then at Carmen.

"I think maybe I should do this caper alone," he said.

"Alone? Are you crazy? You can't go up to that crack alone. You learned that in Police Cadet training. Whenever there is a big risk involved, you need a partner. Well, here I am.

Besides, they are my brother and sister."

"But I can't stand to see you crawling up there across that crack," his voice trembled. And then it got very soft. "Carmen, I care too much about you to see you in danger!"

Sara acted as if she wasn't hearing what Bill was saying. She tiptoed away and left them alone.

"I'm just beginning to feel how much I care for you," Bill said. "Tonight has let me see the real girl. Up until tonight, I just thought of you as a good friend. But I don't think I will ever feel that way again."

"I feel different about you, too, Bill." She put her arms around his waist and rested her cheek against his chest. "But don't you see? It works both ways. I could never stay here and wait for you to go up there alone. In training we learned how to be a support team. That's what I am now —your backup partner."

They were standing there, holding each other, when Sara came quietly back to them.

"Here," she said. "My old clothesline. Tie yourselves together before you start to belly up that old mountain. That way, if one starts to slip, the other can hang on. If I could show you, I would. I used to climb mountains when I was younger. Right up rocky cliffs that make this one look like a peanut."

They started walking up the mountain with

the boards swung over their shoulders. But after Carmen fell down twice, Bill said, "That does it. We've got to take off our heavy clothes and get down on our bellies."

Carmen moaned at the thought, but she stripped to her shirt and pants. So did Bill. She shivered. "The rain is so very cold!" They got down on their bellies and pushed the boards ahead of them. The rope was tied around both of them.

"Ooooooh," Bill said.

"Ugh! Yuck! Ooooooh," moaned Carmen. "Yish!" Then she started to cry. "I just can't do it!" She lay still in the mud.

Bill had his arms around her in a minute. "I can do it alone. Go back."

"No! I'm not going to let you do it alone. Give me a minute! I'll get used to it."

Bill found her muddy mouth, and he kissed her. It was their first kiss. Carmen hung on to it as long as she could. Then he brushed some of the mud off her face. "That was sure a muddy kiss!"

"Best I could do for now," she said with a grin. "But could I have another try when I'm clean and dry?"

"You've got a rain check for it," he said with a laugh as they started moving again. They got closer and closer to the crack.

When they reached the edge, they pushed

the boards across the crack like a bridge. Then they crawled like two big muddy worms over the boards.

On the other side of the crack, they still could not stand up and walk. The mud was as soft as pudding.

They were about ten feet from the tower when the rain began pouring down as if the sky had broken. The mud got so slippery that even on their bellies they had a hard time to keep moving up the mountain. Rocks kept running in the mud, coming down the mountain and hitting them.

"Now I think I am black-and-blue all over," Carmen said. She raised her head. She could see the rain cape and the eight legs not far ahead.

"The twins don't even know we are close to them," she called to Bill, who was so muddy it was hard to see him. "They have that cape over them like a tent."

"Don't call to them yet," Bill said. "We don't want to scare them. They might run."

So they kept on crawling in the mud.

"Oooooh," Carmen moaned. "I'm so cold! And I hurt all over. Why doesn't the rain wash the mud and rocks away from us instead of right onto us?"

Somewhere they heard a loud roar. They felt the earth under their bellies shaking.

"Another slide!" shouted Carmen.

She looked up ahead. They were close enough now to hear the twins.

"They're both crying," she said.

"They're scared. Now we have to be careful. They might not know us, the way we look, covered with mud," Bill said. "We don't want to scare them and make them run up the mountain."

"We must look like muddy monsters," Carmen said. "But they would know my voice."

"Flory!" she called. "Biff!"

They watched the cape shaking and moving around. Then two faces peeked out into the night.

"Carmie! Where are you?" Biff said.

"Carmie! Carmie! Carmie!" Flory cried.

"We'll never be bad again," Biff yelled. "Where are you, Carmie?"

"Look in the mud," she yelled. "Don't be scared. That big muddy thing crawling up is me."

Carmen reached one of the posts that held up the water tower. She pulled herself up. The twins stared at her.

"Oh," Flory said. "Mommy will be mad at you for getting all that mud on you!"

"Yes," said Biff. "She'll put you in the bathtub and scrub you and then make you stay in your room!"

"I hope she does," Carmen said. She was crying. She hugged the twins and got them all muddy.

"How are we going to get home?" Biff asked her.

"You're going to have to sit down on your bottoms," she said, "and let Bill and me slide you down through the mud. It's a game we're playing. You like to play games, don't you?"

They both looked at her and started crying very hard.

"No! Not up here!" they wept together.

13
The Fearful Trip Down

Carmen put her arms around Flory, and Bill put his arms around Biff.

"You must not let go of us, not for even one minute," Carmen warned. "The mountain is very slippery."

They both looked back at the big red dog. He was still wearing the cape and looking at everyone as if he thought they were all crazy.

"We can't go without Catsup," Biff said. "We can't leave him here! He kept us nice and warm."

"He's a real nice dog," Flory said. "We want to take him home with us."

Carmen was looking at the cape.

"Bill, what if we wrap the twins up in the cape and then hold on to them and slide them down to the crack? That way we can keep them warm and dry."

"I'm worried about the crack. I hope we can

still find the place where we left the boards. But if we have the twins rolled up in the cape, it might be easier to get them that far."

"Well, everything is going down the mountain—the water, the mud, and the rocks. It should be easier going down than coming up," Carmen said. She made the twins lie down on the cape.

"This is part of the game," she said. "So you won't get all muddy like me, and Mom won't be mad at you."

"Will we be able to breathe in here?" Biff said.

"Sure," Carmen said. She had them all tucked in tight.

Bill was looking down the mountain. "It is very steep and slippery," he said. "I wish we had some kind of brakes. I don't want to slide down into that crack. I wish I had brought a longer rope. I could have tied it to the tower post and then we could have gone down slowly."

"Well, we can't stretch this rope, so let's start down," Carmen said.

She took one end of the rolled-up cape and Bill took the other. She and Bill scooted on their bottoms. Catsup let out a growl. He sank his teeth into the cape and held on.

"Maybe we do have brakes!" Carmen said. She petted the dog and coaxed him to come along. In a minute he let go of the cape and stepped out into the rain, but he stayed only two inches behind the cape.

"He doesn't trust us," Carmen said as she scooted and slipped. Already her bottom was sore. "This is even worse than crawling on our bellies!"

"You're right," Bill said. "Back on your belly!"

The rain and the mud pushed them down the mountain much faster than they had been able to go up.

Sometimes they could hear the twins crying inside the cape. Other times, they would hear a giggle.

They were getting near the crack when the rain came down even harder.

"I can't see anything," Carmen yelled.

"Neither can I!" Bill said.

The mud rolling down the mountainside began to push them down, down, down. They were being washed toward the crack.

"We have to slow down," Bill yelled.

"Help us, Catsup!" Carmen yelled at the big dog. He was slipping and sliding almost as much as they were. Sometimes he was coming down the mountain sideways. But he looked at her, and his ears went up. He heard the fright in her voice.

Catsup reached down with his teeth and

caught the cape again. He held on very tight. It slowed them down.

"Just in time!" Bill shouted. "The crack is only a few feet from us."

"But where are the boards?" Carmen asked. "I don't see the boards!"

14
Surprise!

"We'd better stay here," Bill said, "until the rain slows down again. We have to be able to see so we can get across that crack."

"I wish I was inside the cape," Carmen said. She lay there with her face pointing down at the mud. "I'm so cold and so tired and so hungry. I wonder if this mud would taste good."

Bill was looking up at the sky. "The rain is not coming down as hard as it was. And, look! The sky is starting to clear."

Carmen looked up. There were light-gray spaces in the black sky. And then she yelled, "Look! The moon! I thought it was gone forever!"

Bill was sitting up. He was looking down at the crack.

"There! Over there! I can see our boards!"

They put the boards side by side. Bill went across with the rope. Carmen held the boards.

Once they had pulled the twins across the crack, they unwrapped them from the cape. It had almost stopped raining.

"Everyone walks from here," Carmen said. "We have to get these boards back to Sara."

The twins thought it was fun, walking and falling in the sticky mud.

"Are you sure Mommy won't be mad?" Biff asked.

Carmen laughed. "She is going to hug and kiss you like you have never been hugged and kissed before."

As they neared Sara's house they smelled bacon frying.

"I'm so hungry I could die!" Carmen said. She ran the last few steps to the car port.

Sara heard them coming. She opened the door. They could see newspapers all over the floors. "I have a hot bath waiting in the bathroom for you and the little girl," she told Carmen. "And Mrs. Bess has some clothes for you."

She turned to Bill. "Mrs. Bess helped me drag my old washtub down from the attic. It's full of hot, soapy water in the bedroom. You and the little boy can bathe in there. I found some of my husband's clothes in the attic. You can put those on. Mrs. Bess has clothes for the little boy."

They hurried across the newspapers and into their hot baths. Nothing ever felt so good to them. They soaked until the water began to cool, and then they put on the fresh clothes. Even Catsup was sprayed clean. He shook himself dry.

When they came out from their baths, all the newspapers were burning brightly in the fireplace and a table was set beside the fire. On it were a big platterful of bacon and eggs and a basket of homemade muffins. Nothing ever tasted so good to them. The twins shared their bacon with the big, hungry dog.

"I'm sorry about the boards," Bill said. "I put them in Dad's car. I'll try to fix them."

Sara shrugged her shoulders. "They served a good purpose," she said.

After they ate, Carmen and Bill put Biff and Flory and Catsup in the car. They waved to Sara, Mrs. Bess, and her sister, and Bill headed carefully down the steep road. Mud and rocks were everywhere, but the rain had stopped at last.

The sky was getting light. Carmen looked up at it. "We walked and ran and crawled all night!"

Then they all listened. They heard the sound of heavy earth-moving machines. The car rounded a bend, and they could see the big yellow machines working to move the mud slide off Snake Road.

"Our dads will be home soon," Carmen said. She was thinking. "Maybe it would be best if we didn't tell them what we did up there. I don't want to be a hero, do you? We don't have to tell anyone how we crawled up the mountain over that crack, or what a bad time we had getting the twins down. We can just say that we found them under the water tower and brought them down to Sara's house."

"That's all right with me," Bill said.

They were passing Mr. Porter's house. He was standing out in the road looking at all the mud.

Bill slowed down. "We found the twins."

Mr. Porter's face was one big smile. "I knew you would! And safe and warm and well." He reached in to pat Biff. He saw the boards.

"Those look like good old oak table boards," he said. "Where did you get those?"

"We had to borrow them from Sara up at the top of the canyon. I'm sorry. We got them a little muddy."

Mr. Porter was pulling them out of the car. "A little muddy! These lovely boards are all scratched and banged up!"

"Well, we had to use them a little hard up there."

Mr. Porter was wiping them off with his handkerchief. "Woodworking is my hobby," he said. "I'll bet I could fix these boards as good as new again. Such lovely oak. Could I try?"

"That would be great," Bill said. "I know you can do a better job than I can."

When they got to Carmen's house, her mother laughed and cried because she was so happy. Carmen said good-by to Bill. Then she and the twins went to bed. She slept until the next day.

"I thought you were never going to wake up," her dad said when she came out of her room.

"I still feel like sleeping some more," she said.

"Not today! It's Saturday afternoon and Captain Hope is holding the meeting this afternoon."

"You mean I'm going to get my Police Cadet pin today?" Carmen said. She was so happy. "I thought the meetings were always held at night."

"They always were. But this time Captain Hope moved the meeting to the high school gym and set it up for this afternoon."

"Why would he hold it in the gym?" Carmen wondered.

"You'll see," her father said.

She could smell a cake baking. It was her

mother's famous "Midnight Cake" that she only baked for very special times.

Carmen could hardly believe the day had come. She and Bill were finally wearing their new uniforms.

They were a little late. Mrs. Chavez had made them late. She kept doing little things that held them up. At the last minute she had taken the twins over to stay with Mrs. Feder.

"They wouldn't sit still at the gym," she said. "And I want to enjoy every minute of it when you get your Police Cadet pin."

Carmen's dad and Bill's dad had gone on to the meeting together. They had left much earlier. Bill was driving the off-road car, and he was taking Carmen and her mom to the meeting. His mom had gone to get his grandma.

While Carmen's mom was inside Mrs. Feder's house with the twins, Bill pulled Carmen over close to him.

"Now, how about that rain check you gave me back there in the mud? We're both as clean as soap and water now."

"Ssssh." Carmen suddenly felt very shy. "Mom might be watching us. Or, she might hear us."

"Are you saying I'm a noisy kisser?" Bill teased.

"No," she grinned. "You're the best kisser I ever kissed."

"Oh, I suppose you have been going around kissing a lot of guys. You want to see who can kiss the best?"

"No," she laughed. "You were the first and the best."

They both looked at Mrs. Feder's house. All the drapes were closed.

Then Carmen held out her arms and Bill pulled her into his and they kissed. It was very sweet and wonderful, Carmen thought, but too short. It was cut off because she pulled away when she heard Mrs. Feder's door start to open.

Mrs. Chavez came out the door and walked down to the car. Bill started it, and they drove to the gym. When they got there, they were surprised to find it jammed with people.

Carmen looked up at the stage and she couldn't believe her eyes. She expected to see Captain Hope, Bill's dad, and her dad up there.

Instead she saw Mrs. Feder with Susie and the twins, Sara with Mrs. Bess and Mrs. Bess's sister, Mr. Porter and Pink Eye, and Catsup! Dr. Gibson was standing on the steps to the stage.

While she was staring at all of them, Captain Hope walked in. After him came her dad and the Chief of Police! And then Bill's dad walked in with the Mayor.

Carmen looked at Bill. "What is happening here today besides our getting our pins?"

"I wish I knew," he said. "I hope it doesn't take all afternoon. I'm still tired."

"So am I," Carmen said.

Captain Hope asked Mrs. Feder to speak. "I was going out of my head because of the storm," she said. "I think I would have gone crazy if Carmen and Bill hadn't come to my house and calmed me."

Then she told almost everything that had happened at her house on that afternoon of the mud slides.

When she was through talking, Captain Hope asked Mr. Porter and Pink Eye to tell what had happened at Mr. Porter's house.

"Ooooooh," Carmen said, sliding down in her seat. "I wish all these people would stop blabbing!"

"Me too," Bill said. "For Pete's sake, we only did what we had to. There was no one else there to do it."

Mrs. Bess told everything that had happened until she got to Sara's house. Then Sara took over and told the rest of the story.

"But no one is going to be able to tell what it felt like bellying up that mountain in the mud," Carmen whispered to Bill. He reached over and held her hand.

At last the twins stood up and told how Carmen and Bill brought them down the mountain. They had to be coaxed by their dad to keep talking. Twice Flory got the giggles.

"Well, at least Catsup can't talk!" Carmen said.

"I wouldn't bet on it," groaned Bill. "I wish I was still on top of the mountain!"

All Catsup said was, "Arf!" and he wagged his tail.

Captain Hope asked if anyone in the gym knew who owned the dog. No one did.

"Then I guess Flory and Biff can keep Catsup for their own," he said.

The twins hugged the dog, and Flory kissed him on the nose. Catsup wagged his tail faster and faster.

The Chief of Police stood up, then, and called out, "Carmen Chavez and Bill Parker, please come forward."

Carmen's knees were shaking as she walked up onto the stage. The Chief of Police handed the pin to her dad and he pinned it on her shirt. She had never felt so happy before in her life.

Next Bill's dad did the same for him. After the two were pinned, the Chief and the Mayor and Captain Hope shook their hands. The Chief said, "Welcome to the police force. We need good people like you!"

It was then that Dr. Gibson walked up onto the stage. "I want all you people out there, especially you high school students who came to school on a free day, to know how proud I am to have Bill and Carmen in my school. Now, let's show Bill and Carmen how we feel."

They didn't just clap. They whistled. They stamped their feet. Some of them shouted, "Carmen and Bill!"

"You know," Dr. Gibson went on, "just a few days ago I was afraid that the other kids would resent having two Police Cadets on our campus. I was afraid it would cause a problem for Carmen and Bill. Was I right or wrong?"

The shout "Wrong" was like a roar.

Carmen looked out over the crowd. Way back by the door she saw Lisa and Tom. She wondered why Lisa was carrying an umbrella when the sun was shining outside—at last.

Then the Mayor stepped up to Carmen and Bill.

"There's just one more thing," the Mayor said. And, stepping forward, he gave each of them a badge for bravery. "All of Larks Canyon thanks you," he said. "And so does the city. Fifty-five families were shut off in the canyon during that bad storm. They had no police or firemen. But they had two Police Cadets who did a very good job! You not only found Flory and Biff but you lent a helping hand wherever it was needed, while you went on with your search!"

At last all the hand-shaking was over.

"All I want to do is hurry home, eat some of Mom's cake," Carmen said to Bill, "and take another nap. I'm still pooped. How about you?"

"Same here. Come on. Let's try to sneak out before anyone else decides to stop us."

They moved toward a side door, but they had gone only a few steps when Tom and Lisa walked up to them. Lisa handed Carmen the umbrella. It was a brand-new one. And it was much better than the one that Lisa had jumped on.

"Here!" she said. "I want you to have this!"

"But you didn't have to," Carmen said. "I had other umbrellas."

"That's all right," Lisa said. "Have one from me!"

Then she and Tom started to move away from Carmen, but Carmen caught up to them.

"Instead of this umbrella," she said, "do you know what I would rather have?"

Lisa looked at Carmen and nodded her head. "You want us to give up dust."

Carmen nodded.

"We aren't making any promises," Lisa said,

and she and Tom walked away very fast.

Just then someone touched Carmen's arm. It was Pink Eye.

"Can I ask you something?" he said.

She nodded.

"Well, I've been thinking," Pink Eye said. "I want to be a Police Cadet too. How do I start?"

So, instead of going home to the cake, Bill and Carmen went to Captain Hope's office, got out the papers for Pink Eye, and helped him sign up.

About the Author

ROSEMARY BRECKLER studied journalism at Ohio State University and magazine editing and TV writing at Valley Community College in Van Nuys, California.

Ms. Breckler has served as editor and staff writer for California newspapers and magazines and as an account executive. She is now a private investigator and free-lance writer.

As a private investigator she has worked on some sensational homicide cases and has worked undercover on many cases. As an undercover agent she traveled to Central America on a Russian ship.

Ms. Breckler has served in the Armed Forces and, as secretary to the Inspector General, Fifth Service Command, U.S. Army, worked on investigations.

She is an award-winning reporter. Her reports cover earthquakes, environmental crises,

UFO's, search and rescue stories when she was with the U.S. Coast Guard Auxiliary, and she once lived on an Indian reservation to cover the Centennial Pow-Wow.

As a Girl Scout leader, recruiter, and trainer, she has worked with young people and has written and directed many small plays and musical comedies for teen-agers.